Pearlie and the Fairy Queen

WENDY HARMER

Illustrated by Gypsy Taylor

RANDOM HOUSE AUSTRALIA

For my enchanting sister, Helen.

A Random House book
Published by Random House Australia Pty Ltd
Level 3, 100 Pacific Highway, North Sydney NSW 2060
www.randomhouse.com.au

First published by Random House Australia in 2008

Addresses for companies within the Random House Group can be found at
www.randomhouse.com.au/offices.

National Library of Australia
Cataloguing-in-Publication Entry

   Harmer, Wendy.
     Pearlie and the fairy queen/author, Wendy Harmer; illustrator, Gypsy Taylor.
     ISBN 978 1 74166 149 1 (pbk).
     Series: Pearlie; 10
     For primary school age.
     Fairies – Juvenile fiction.
     Other Authors/contributors: Taylor, Gypsy.

   A823.4

Designed and typeset by Jobi Murphy
Printed and bound by Sing Cheong Printing Co. Ltd, Hong Kong

10 9 8 7 6 5 4 3 2 1

It was dawn on a fine spring day in Jubilee Park. Pearlie the Park Fairy had been flitting about, fluffing flowers, polishing leaves and making extra sure that everything was in its place, just right.

She was sitting down to morning tea with her two best friends, Opal the Desert Fairy and Jasper the Elf, when outside her door she saw a very unusual sight indeed. It was a magnificent ladybird with golden wings and jewelled spots that glittered in the sun. Pearlie had never seen a creature quite like it.

'Good morning,' whispered the ladybird. 'I have a message to deliver to Pearlie the Park Fairy.'

'That's me!' said Pearlie.

The ladybird rummaged in its bag and found a scroll decorated with sparkling tassels. Pearlie unrolled the silvery paper and this is what it said:

Her Majesty Queen Emerald, ~most magical monarch of Fairyland~ will visit Jubilee Park at dusk today for a very important announcement.

'Stars and Moonbeams!' exclaimed Pearlie.
'Crikey!' said Opal.
'Cool,' said Jasper.

'And,' said the ladybird, 'Queen Emerald
would like to have supper with you in your
famous pink shell.'

Pearlie kindly thanked the ladybird and off it flew. Pearlie read the scroll once more and could not believe it. The Fairy Queen had never visited Jubilee Park before.

'I'll bet you are going to be crowned Fairy of the Year,' said Opal.

'ME? Fairy of the Year?' gasped Pearlie. 'Do you really think so?'

'Way to go, dude!' Jasper clapped his hands with excitement.

Pearlie looked around her shell. It was, as usual, an awful mess. 'Roots and twigs!' said Pearlie as she tied on her apron. 'If Queen Emerald is coming to supper, I've got cakes to bake and things to dust. I'd better get started.'

Opal and Jasper flew off to give the news to all the creatures of Jubilee Park. Soon Brush and Sugar Possum, Mother Duck and her ducklings, Silky and Sulky and the four frogs were all gathered under the Jacaranda tree.

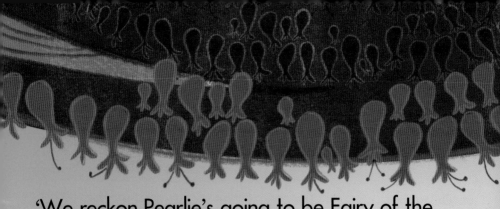

'We reckon Pearlie's going to be Fairy of the Year,' said Opal proudly. 'And I bet the prize will be something magnificent.'

Everyone was thrilled.

'And Queen Emerald's coming to visit.'

AARGH! EEK, RIBBIT, WAKKA WAK, OOOH! Everyone shouted, ran this way and that and disappeared in a twinkling. They had a lot of work to do to prepare for the Queen's visit.

Opal and Jasper thought they'd also better get ready for the grand occasion and they raced away.

However, no-one in Jubilee Park knew that those two scabby rodents – Scrag and Mr Flea – had been watching everything from behind a bush.

'Wait till Miss Sapphire hears about this!' cackled Scrag, and off they scurried to Sapphire's place at the bottom of the garden.

Sapphire was furious.

'IT'S NOT FAIR!!' she wailed and stamped her pointy black boots. 'I should be Fairy of the Year! I want to have supper with Queen Emerald!'

Then Sapphire had a very sneaky idea. 'Perhaps it's time to pay dear Great Aunt Garnet a visit!' she giggled naughtily.

'If we come with you, can we have a treat?' asked Scrag.

'Smelly cheese on a stick! Mouldy crusts in batter! Yum!' said Mr Flea, rubbing his fat hairy gut.

'When I'm Fairy of the Year you will have treats EVERY day,' said Sapphire with a wicked smile.

All afternoon everyone in Jubilee Park worked hard to make it picture perfect.

Jasper re-painted his letterbox.

Opal swept her desert garden.

The frogs decorated their lily pads.

Silky and Sulky spun
a web fit for a Queen.

Brush and Sugar possum
hung garlands of gumnuts.

Mother Duck scrubbed
her nest and her ducklings
until they sparkled.

Back in her shell, Pearlie was as busy as a bee. As she dusted and tidied and baked she practised her royal greeting.

'Good evening, your magical royalness … um …'

'Hello there, Queen Emerald, your most majesty … er …'

'Twirly-whirly!' said Pearlie. She was starting to feel quite nervous.

Meanwhile, Sapphire and the rats had arrived at Great Aunt Garnet's shop behind the old clock tower.

'Hello, Great Aunt Garnet,' she said sweetly.

Why, young Sapphire, what a surprise!
Can I see mischief in your pretty blue eyes?

'Oh no!' said Sapphire. 'I hear Pearlie might be Fairy of the Year. Isn't that wonderful? I'd like to give her a present of a lovely scarf.'

Well, well, well, how nice of you.
Now, what colour do you think — pink or blue?

'I think Pearlie would like an orange one with jacaranda blue spots and a silky fringe,' said Sapphire. 'Do you have one down the back?'

I might just have one in that big pile.
I'll go and fetch it ... I might be a while.

As soon as Great Aunt Garnet had gone to
search for the gift, Scrag and Mr Flea scrabbled
over the front counter and began ransacking
her cupboards.

'Hurry up will you!' snarled Sapphire.

Soon the rats found what they were looking
for. They came back with a mysterious jar of
twinkling purple dust. Sapphire pushed them out
the door and followed, laughing all the way.

When Great Aunt Garnet came back with the special scarf, she was most surprised to see her customer had disappeared.

Sapphire is up to something today!
Could it be because the Queen is coming this way?

Back in her shell, Pearlie was putting the finishing touches to the royal supper. She had made rose petal muffins, fairy bread, sunflower snap biscuits, dew drop jellies and jugs of daisy fizz. Everything was perfect!

Pearlie was just about to get dressed in her best gown when a cloud of strange purple dust came swirling through her front door.

'Reeds and ripples, that looks like … yawn!' sighed Pearlie. She suddenly felt very tired indeed. 'Oh, I think I might take a little … nap … zzzzz.' Pearlie fell on her bed and was fast asleep.

It was dusk in Jubilee Park. Everyone was
gathered at the fairy ring and looking their very
best. They were most excited to be meeting the
Queen of Fairyland!

Four fabulous butterflies sounded flowery
trumpets to herald the arrival of Her Majesty.

Across the sky came a flight of jewelled ladybirds two by two. Behind them, in a cloud of rainbow fairy dust and wearing a shimmering green gown and splendid crown, came Her Royal Highness, Queen Emerald of Fairyland. Her hair shone ruby-red in the afternoon sun.

'Good evening, dear friends,' said the Queen. Her voice sounded like summer rain on rose petals.

'Good evening, your majesty,' everyone said and curtsied. (At this point two ducklings fell over, but thankfully the Queen didn't seem to notice.)

'Now, would Pearlie the Park Fairy please step forward.'

Well, this was embarrassing! No-one knew where Pearlie was. She was never late. Imagine keeping the Fairy Queen waiting!

'Is Pearlie not here?' asked the Queen kindly. 'I was very much looking forward to meeting her.'

Everyone started to whisper. Where was Pearlie?

'ERK! CROAK. Here she comes!' called the frogs. Pearlie came flying at a great rate. She landed in front of the Queen with a bump.

'Phew! Got here,' said Pearlie.

'Hmmm,' said Queen Emerald. 'You are rather late.'

'I don't think I was late. I think you were early,' Pearlie replied.

Everyone gasped. How rude! Queen Emerald just smiled graciously and held a tiny tiara above Pearlie's head.

'As Queen of Fairyland, it is my great honour to pronounce you Fairy of the–'

'Yes, I know all that,' said Pearlie, 'Come on! Where's my prize?'

OOOH!

That was even ruder! Everyone was shocked. This wasn't at all like Pearlie.

Just then, the youngest duckling, who had climbed on top of a toadstool to get a better look, tumbled and fell on top of Pearlie. Down he went in a tangle of necklaces and long silvery hair. And, when everyone looked up … there stood Sapphire!

ERRR!

She had disguised herself as Pearlie and fooled everyone! Queen Emerald was most displeased. She zapped Sapphire with her wand. Sapphire's wings immediately shrivelled up and fell off! They would take a whole year to grow back. Sapphire stomped off to the bottom of the garden. It was a very long walk.

Then Great Aunt Garnet appeared.

Come now, Queen Em, please follow me.
I think I've solved the mystery.

'My dearest Garnet!' laughed Queen Emerald.
'Do lead the way.'

When the Queen stepped inside, she saw that every scrap of food had been eaten. Those greedy, beastly rats had got away again!

They had given poor Pearlie magic sleeping dust and she had slept through it all. Queen Emerald used her wand to cast a fairy rainbow in the room and began to sing. It was the most enchanting song anyone had ever heard.

Wake up, Pearlie, Fairy of the Year!
Open your eyes and shine, my dear.
All good things are waiting here,
For you sweet Pearlie, our Fairy of the Year!

Pearlie woke and rubbed her eyes. She couldn't believe who was standing in front of her.

Queen Emerald took Pearlie's hand and flew her to the fairy ring where everyone was waiting.

'You are kind, loving and care for every living thing. We are so proud of you,' said the Queen. She placed the tiara on Pearlie's head. (It matched quite nicely with her apron!)

Everyone gave their favourite fairy three hearty cheers. HIP, HIP, HOORAY, HOORAY, HOORAY!

Opal and Jasper hugged each other. They were so happy for their dear friend.

'My special gift to you is an invitation to visit all the other Park Fairies in the world,' said Queen Emerald. 'My ladybirds-in-waiting will pack your things and we'll leave after supper. Butterflies — if you please.'

The butterflies flitted about and had soon laid a sweet feast on toadstool tables – crystal jugs of nectar fizz, sugar-coated daisy petals, pollen puffs and, of course, dainty butterfly cakes.

It was almost dawn when everyone had eaten and drunk every last morsel. Queen Emerald then turned to Pearlie. 'Come, my dear, now it's time for us to go.'

Pearlie kissed her friends goodbye, with special hugs for Opal, Jasper and Great Aunt Garnet. She took Queen Emerald's hand.

'Hurly-burly,' said Pearlie with a tear in her eye. 'I'll miss all of you. I'm sure I'll see you soon.'

'And so you shall,' said the Queen.

Then Queen Emerald and Pearlie climbed aboard jewelled ladybirds and took to the sky.